The Junior Novelization

 Published in the United States by Random House Children's Books, a division of Random House, Inc., 1745 Broadway, New York, NY 10019, and in Canada by Random House of Canada Limited, Toronto, in conjunction with Disney Enterprises, Inc. Random House and the colophon are registered trademarks of Random House, Inc.
Library of Congress Control Number: 2009943515
ISBN: 978-0-7364-2689-3
www.randomhouse.com/kids
Printed in the United States of America
10 9 8 7 6 5 4 3 2 1

The Junior Novelization

Adapted by Kimberly Morris

Random House  New York

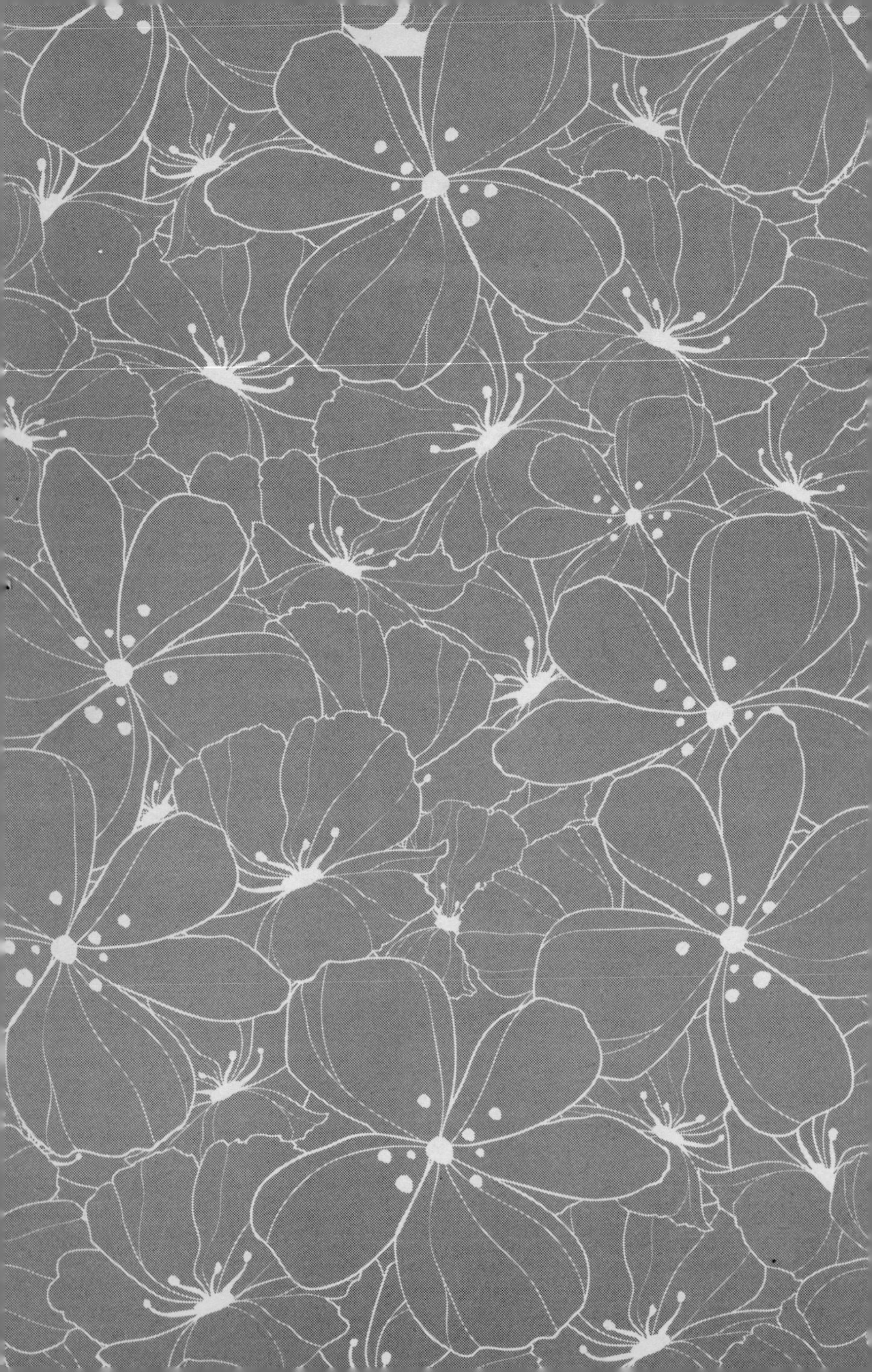

One

Tinker Bell sailed happily through the clouds. Close behind were her friends Rosetta, Silvermist, Iridessa, and Fawn. "Whoa! Look at that!" cried Silvermist, pointing toward the mainland below. Somewhere down there, hidden from human view, was the place where the fairies would spend the summer.

As they approached, Tink kept her eyes peeled for Terence. Terence was Tinker Bell's best friend. She swooped to meet him, and he gave her an affectionate grin. "Hey, Tink! Ready for your first summer on the mainland?"

"Absolutely," Tink answered. "It's so beautiful out here. I can't believe we get to stay for the whole season."

"Well, what are we waiting for?" Terence teased.

Tinker Bell didn't pause for a moment. She zoomed down toward the countryside, with Terence doing his best to keep up.

This was Tink's first summer season change. But luckily her friends had done it many times before and already knew the ropes.

Rosetta the garden fairy flew away from the group and hovered next to some flowers. A swarm of bees raced out of the trees and began feasting on the flowers' nectar. One little bee got crowded out and couldn't find a place. Rosetta guided him to an open flower where he could drink his fill.

Iridessa the light fairy flew to a heavily shaded area of a nearby glen. The sunflowers there looked sad and droopy. Iridessa adjusted a swatch of sunlight so that its warm rays shone directly on the limp flowers. Immediately, they perked up and turned their wide golden faces to the sky.

Fawn the animal fairy greeted a little bird with open arms. And Silvermist the water fairy zoomed past a couple of frogs and their pollywogs sitting on a fallen tree trunk on the bank of a stream. "Hi, guys!" she shouted, flying just above the water. The pollywogs spotted their fairy friend and jumped along after her.

Out in a field, Vidia, the fastest of the fast-flying fairies, was hard at work. Tinker Bell saw her flying over the ground, creating a strong wind. Every blade of grass woke up and joyfully swayed in her wake.

Tinker Bell had never felt so happy. When she'd first arrived in Pixie Hollow, the tinker fairies weren't allowed to go to the mainland. Only the nature fairies were allowed to participate in the changing of the seasons.

Tinker Bell didn't like that arrangement at all. So she decided to show everyone that the tinker fairies were just as important to the process as the nature fairies.

The result: Tinker fairies were now a permanent part of the season change team.

This season change—spring to summer—involved a

three-month trip. That meant that the tinker fairies weren't just important, they were essential. If the fairies were going to spend three months living and working on the mainland, equipment would break, contraptions would backfire, and problems would crop up that required on-site tinkering.

No doubt about it, Tinker Bell expected to be very busy this summer.

During the past two season changes, Tinker Bell had gotten herself into all kinds of trouble.

Each time, though, she had landed on her feet—and even bounced a bit.

She vowed that this season would be different.

There would be no mistakes.

No mishaps.

No accidents.

She would do her job and not cause one teeny tiny, itsy bitsy, little bitty bit of trouble.

Not even a smidge.

Two

Terence led Tinker Bell over a ridge toward a tall tree. "There it is, Tink. Fairy camp!" A fairy on the ground waved mushroom caps to guide them to the landing field. Tink and Terence touched down in the center of a ring of toadstools.

A whistle from above warned them that something large was coming in for a landing. They looked up and saw a bird with a big carrier on his back. *Aha!* Tinker Bell smiled happily, eager to take delivery of this cargo.

The bird circled expertly down. Once he was safely on the ground, Tinker Bell raced forward and opened the carrier. Out sprang Cheese, Tink's cart-pulling mouse and trusted working buddy.

Cheese was as happy to see Tink as she was to see

him. He pressed his soft pink nose against her cheek. Tink returned his kiss with a hug. "Hiya, Cheese. Did you have a nice flight?"

Cheese squeaked happily and scurried away. Next out of the carrier came Blaze the firefly. He woozily wobbled onto the grass, his little face looking green.

"Aw, Blaze," said Tink, her voice full of sympathy. "Did you get airsick?"

Blaze's buzz was affirmative.

Tink wanted to make sure Blaze was okay before she did more exploring with Terence. When she saw the firefly happily eating some fruit, she knew it was safe to leave him.

Tinker Bell was excited to be on the mainland, but she was also surprised there weren't more fairies around. "Tink, fairy camp isn't out here," Terence explained. He walked over to a large patch of undergrowth beneath a massive oak tree. He pulled a leafy curtain aside and Tinker Bell gasped.

Everywhere Tinker Bell looked, she saw fairies in motion.

"Wow! It's like all of Pixie Hollow under one tree," she marveled.

Terence nodded proudly, clearly enjoying his role as tour guide. "Summer's our busiest season. That's why we have this base camp, so we can go out every day to bring summer to life."

As they walked through the camp, Terence handed out sacks. "Ready for your pixie dust?" he asked a passing fairy. She nodded and he handed her a sack. "Here you go."

Tinker Bell was surprised at Terence's generous rationing of the precious pixie dust. Back in Pixie Hollow, where they lived, each fairy got one teacup of fairy dust a day. Not a speck less, and not a speck more.

But here, clearly, the fairies who traveled away from base camp, or who needed to transport things, received an extra supply.

Terence and Tink passed a bee fairy using a spinning gadget to paint stripes on the bees. The bees were lined up and moving quickly through the bee striping assembly line.

"How's the bee striper working? Need any tweaks?" she asked the bee fairy. Tink was itching to be a part of the action.

The bee fairy shook her head. "It's working fine, Tink. Thanks."

Tink spotted a couple of garden fairies shuttling flower bulbs in a pedal wagon that the tinkers had devised. One of the bulbs jumped out of the wagon and made a run for it.

A garden fairy hurried after it. "Hey! Come back here," she laughed.

"Does your bulbmobile need a tune-up?" Tink asked.

"Nope!" the garden fairy answered. "It's running great."

Tinker Bell kicked the ground and blew her bangs up in frustration.

Terence laughed. "Tink! Everyone just got here," he

explained to his friend. "So nothing's broken yet."

"I just can't wait to start tinkering."

"Don't worry, Tink. You'll find something to fix." He put a hand on her shoulder. "All right! I've got to take pixie dust to the other fairy camps. I'll see you in a couple of days." He started away, then stopped. "Oh, I almost forgot! Here you go, Tink." He tossed her a bag of pixie dust and flew away.

Tinker Bell caught the bag and watched him go. She couldn't help wishing he didn't have to hurry off. In all the hustle and bustle, she felt a bit lost—unsure how or where to begin.

She wandered away to where Fawn and the other girls were already occupied with camp chores. No one appeared to need any help. "Well," Tink said finally, "if there's nothing to fix, I'm going to go look for Lost Things." And off she went.

Lost Things were items from the human world. They

were called Lost Things because fairies only found them when humans lost them.

Tinker Bell was fascinated with Lost Things. They were mysterious and odd. And they gave her lots of good ideas.

Though sometimes, Tinker Bell had to admit, what seemed like a good idea to her didn't seem like a good idea to others.

Three

Poof! A gust of wind blew in, and there stood Vidia, the fastest of the fast-flying fairies.

"Hold on, Little Miss Spare Parts!" Vidia said in her sarcastic voice. "You're not going near the human house, are you?"

Tinker Bell's ears pricked up. "There's a *human house*?"

Rosetta kissed the petals of a sleepy flower bud, and it blossomed into life. "Now, Vidia," Rosetta asked, "don't you think Tinker Bell knows better than that?"

Vidia's brows went up. "Have you *met* Tinker Bell?" she asked.

Iridessa screwed a "bulb" of light into a flower bud, and it glowed with new life. "Tink knows we have to steer clear of the humans or we won't be able to get our work done. Right, Tink?" Iridessa said.

"Right," Tinker Bell agreed. "But . . . then again . . ." Tinker Bell tried to think of some way of making a promise without actually making a promise.

She liked human things.

Vidia threw up her hands in disgust. "Ugh. It's going to be a long summer." She flew off in a blur, as quickly as she had arrived.

"Grouchy," Silvermist commented.

"Oh, that's just Vidia being Vidia," Iridessa responded.

"No," Silvermist said. "The air. The air smells grouchy."

"You can smell the weather?"

"Yes," Silvermist said. "Sometimes it smells happy. Sometimes mad. And right now, it smells grouchy. We might be in for a storm."

Fawn came flitting over to help some nearby fairies paint butterfly wings. "Come on, Sil," she argued. "The sun is shining. The air is warm. It's a beautiful day. Nothing's going to—"

Hooooonk!

Whatever Fawn was about to say was drowned out by a loud and piercing sound.

Everybody jumped, and Fawn was so startled that she splashed paint all over the unpainted wing of a butterfly. The half-painted butterfly flew away, spooked by the noise and Fawn's reaction.

"Ohhhh!" Fawn groaned in frustration.

Before anyone could say a word or ask any questions, a scout fairy came whizzing overhead, blowing his horn. That was the signal that humans were coming and everyone needed to hide.

In front of Tink's eyes, the entire scene seemed to vanish into thin air. Fairies disappeared, along with their tools, behind twigs, blossoms, leaves, and flowers.

Tinker Bell, however, was too curious to resist the

temptation to see what was happening. Instead of going into hiding, she poked her head up through the foliage and stared at the road, determined to know who, or what, had made that grand and explosive sound.

Hoooooonk!

Tinker Bell's eyes widened as the noise grew louder, coming around the bend. Then, suddenly, the thing appeared.

Four

The driver was a man. Beside him was a little girl.

Tinker Bell guessed that the little girl was about eight years old. There was no top on the automobile, so Tinker Bell was able to hear their conversation.

"Thank goodness we're here, Father. It's just like I remember it," said the little girl.

The man smiled. "Yes, Lizzy. Same as last year."

Tinker Bell was amazed by the car. *Wow!* What a contraption. What made it go, she wondered?

The man got out and opened the back of the automobile. The lid popped up like the top of a treasure chest. Tinker Bell peered down, curious to see what was inside.

Sadly, there were no gold coins or jewels. Just an

assortment of big leather boxes with handles.

"I wish it was summer *all year long*!" the little girl shouted happily. She jumped out of the car and dashed into the house, practically falling over a grumpy-looking cat. "Sorry about that, Mr. Twitches," she said with a laugh.

Lizzy's father struggled with the large suitcases, lugging them into the house.

Tinker Bell quickly forgot about the humans. What she really wanted was a good look at this thingamabob.

She flew toward the car and zoomed underneath it. Very ingenious. Tink was impressed.

Just as she was about to dive into the greasy guts and really take a good look, Vidia popped up in front of her. "Tinker Bell. *What* are you doing?"

"Vidia!" Tinker Bell sighed. "This is amazing. It's a carriage that moves by itself. It's a horseless carriage. Do you want to know how it works?"

"Not really."

"So do I!" Tinker Bell was too excited to listen properly. She flew under the car to investigate. "I think this is the part that powers the whole thing. Let me know if it does anything." Tink pulled the intriguing lever.

Splash!

Vidia was dripping wet—and not very happy about it. But before she could say anything else, they heard the creak of a door. Lizzy and her father came ambling out of the house, heading back toward the automobile.

Both Tinker Bell and Vidia froze, knowing that their best chance of not being seen was to hold perfectly still. To the human eye, their wings and costumes would blend right into the background.

"Father, can we bring our tea and scones outside and have them here in the yard? It would be just like a little picnic."

"Not just now, Lizzy. I still have to get the suitcases unpacked and the house settled."

Just then, Tinker Bell saw an old friend from fairy camp—the butterfly that had been startled by the car horn. With its half-painted wings, it didn't look anything like other butterflies.

It came to rest on Lizzy's index finger. "Father, look! What a magnificent butterfly."

The father blinked in surprise and came closer for a better view. "My word! Absolutely astonishing."

"It's so beautiful," Lizzy breathed. "What kind of butterfly is it?"

"Judging from an epidermal membrane, it's clearly an *Apatura iris*. But the wings have two entirely different patterns. That's . . . nearly impossible."

Lizzy smiled. "Well, I guess that's just the way the fairies decided to paint it."

"Lizzy," her father chuckled, "fairies do not paint butterfly wings. Because, as you know, fairies are not real."

Tinker Bell drew in her breath with a gasp. *Not real?* What nonsense!

Tinker Bell watched as the man produced a pen and a journal from his pocket and began to sketch the butterfly.

"It does look like paint dripped on its wing," the little girl insisted.

"Really, Lizzy. Rational people consider a belief in fairies to be quite . . . foolish."

Enough was enough. It was time to teach Mr. Know-It-All a lesson. She would fly around his head, do a series of figure eights, and then land right on his nose.

But just as she was about to take off, Vidia grabbed the back of her dress and held on tight.

The man's eyes moved back and forth between the butterfly and his sketch. "The wings are so fresh. Its chrysalis must have been in the meadow."

"The meadow! Oh, Father, that's where I am going. Would you like to come?" The butterfly fluttered away as the little girl walked to the car. She reached into the trunk and pulled out something large.

The father responded with a preoccupied tone. "Not now, Lizzy. I have to update my field journal for my meeting tomorrow."

Tinker Bell watched Lizzy run off alone into the meadow, carrying her mysterious package.

"Have fun," the father said as he wandered off after the butterfly.

Five

As soon as the humans had gone, Tinker Bell popped up and spread her wings. "All clear. Come on, Vidia."

But Vidia remained on the ground. "I can't fly. My wings are wet."

Tinker Bell touched down beside her. "Oh! That's right. Sorry! Guess you'll have to walk back. But don't worry, I'll keep you company."

Tinker Bell tried to walk beside Vidia, but she was so full of enthusiasm, it was hard to keep her feet on the ground. So she flitted and flew around Vidia as they traveled.

Tink's efforts just seemed to irritate Vidia. "Tinker Bell, maybe if you spent less time causing disasters, you wouldn't have to *help* everybody so much."

Tinker Bell hadn't even heard Vidia's cutting remark. Her eyes had spotted something gleaming on the ground. A button from a human's shirt. She flew past Vidia and picked it up. "Look!"

Vidia rolled her eyes. "So?"

Tinker Bell spotted another button. And another. "We can use these back at camp." She eagerly spun around. "Wow! These will be perfect for the new wagon prototype I've been working on."

One by one, Tink picked up buttons and handed them to Vidia. "I bet if I took two or three and tied them together, I could make one really strong wheel. It's a good thing we're walking or we might never have seen these."

She turned and saw that Vidia's hands were empty. "Hey!" Tink looked past Vidia and saw a button trail. Vidia had tossed them, one by one, back on the ground.

Vidia folded her arms. "Tinker Bell. I'm not carrying this human junk back to camp."

But again, Tinker Bell hardly heard her. She had caught sight of something else. Something totally, indescribably, unbelievably *unbelievable*!

Vidia continued heading down the path that led to the fairy camp, while Tinker Bell charged in a completely different direction, determined to check out what she had just spotted.

It was a house. A tiny house. A house that was exactly the right size for a fairy.

Tinker Bell started toward it.

Meanwhile, Vidia had turned her head and seen Tink headed for trouble.

Once again, Tink felt a hand grab the back of her dress. "Tinker Bell, we're not supposed to go near human houses!" Vidia warned. She ran nervously behind Tink. "Please tell me you're not going in there."

Tinker Bell thought it was funny that, for once, brave and fearless Vidia was scared and she wasn't. It made Tink feel good to be braver than Vidia. She pushed the door open and stepped inside. She could hear Vidia muttering, "She went in there!"

Tinker Bell clapped with delight when she saw a dented upside-down thimble made into a table. Whoever had designed this house was somebody who thought like a tinker fairy.

She picked up a tiny mint from a candy dish and was just about to pop it into her mouth when Vidia's voice brought her up short. "Tinker Bell, don't eat that! This could be a trap!"

Tinker Bell turned and saw Vidia framed in the doorway, looking at the inside of the house as if she expected snakes to come dropping from the ceiling.

"Oh, come on, Vidia. It's perfectly safe."

"Oh, really?" Vidia tested her wings, which were dry now, and began to twirl. She raised a small whirlwind that caused the door to slam shut.

"Not so safe now, is it?" Vidia asked from outside the door.

"Nice try, Vidia. But you're not scaring me." Tinker Bell went to check out a fairy-sized clock. Unable to resist, she reached forward and fiddled with the hands. "Gosh! This thing is amazing."

"You just don't know when to stop, do you?" Vidia's voice sounded muffled and small outside the door.

Tinker Bell heard the loud snap of a twig. Then she heard Vidia struggling with the door. "Tink! Someone's coming and the door is stuck."

Tink rolled her eyes. "Oh, come on, Vidia. You can do better than that."

"Tink, I'm serious," Vidia insisted. "Get out of there."

"Just a second, just a second." Tink wasn't going to give Vidia the satisfaction of hurrying. After thoroughly admiring the inner workings of the clock, she went to the door and turned the handle. It wouldn't open. She jiggled the doorknob. “Oh, Vidia, come on. Open the door. You’ve had your fun.”

But there was an eerie silence outside the door.

Tinker Bell rattled the doorknob insistently, beginning to feel nervous in spite of herself. “Okay, Vidia. Not funny anymore.”

Suddenly, a giant shadow fell over Tink. Something was blocking the window. Tink turned and saw a giant eyeball looking in.

Tinker Bell shrieked and the giant eyeball grew large, as if whoever was peeking in was just as surprised to see her.

Tinker Bell heard a voice outside the house. Lizzy’s voice. “A . . . a . . . fairy!” she cried. “A real fairy!”

The next thing Tink knew, the house was being lifted into the air as if by a cyclone. Tink was thrown from one wall to the other as Lizzy ran through the meadow carrying the house. “Father!” Lizzy shouted. “Father! Father!”

Tinker Bell held on as tight as she could and groaned.

She had a bad feeling. The kind of feeling you get when you know you're in trouble.

Not just a smidge of trouble.

Big trouble.

Six

Vidia chased Lizzy through the meadow and back to the house. Unfortunately, Lizzy got to the door ahead of her and kicked it shut, slamming it in Vidia's face.

Vidia peeled off and began checking the windows, flying from one to the other, hoping to find one open.

She found a window that was open just a crack. On the other side of the glass, she could see the little girl's father. He sat at a desk with his journal and looked very busy.

Lizzy ran into the room. "Father!"

"Yes, Lizzy."

"You're never going to believe what I've found." Lizzy plopped the fairy house on the desk.

"Maybe later, Lizzy," he said.

"But, Father—"

"Just a moment, dear. I'm very busy with my project."

The little girl shifted from one foot to the other in her impatience. "But, Father—"

"Lizzy, please. I am just adding this extraordinary discovery to my field journal." He scribbled quickly and finished with a flourish. "And here it is." He put down the pen and held up the journal so she could see. He had drawn a very detailed picture of the butterfly.

"Is that the butterfly we were looking at earlier?" she asked, her voice uneasy.

"Yes. Quite a specimen, isn't it?"

"You're not going to take it to London, are you?"

"Yes, of course. The Board of Regents would never believe me if they didn't see it themselves. Now I'm sure to get that curatorship at the museum."

Vidia watched the little girl's eyes move up to the walls of the room. It was lined with boxes in which lots of beautiful butterflies had been mounted for display, with pins.

"As a member of the scientific community, I'm obligated to share significant findings like this with my colleagues. I know it's unfortunate for the specimen, but really, there is no other way," said Dr. Griffiths. "Now, what did you want to see me about?"

Vidia's stomach churned. If this man got hold of Tinker Bell, would she wind up in one of those boxes, too?

It was clear that the same thought was dawning on Lizzy. Her eyes were sad and full of worry. She moved the fairy house slightly and held it behind her. "Um . . . never mind."

Lizzy exited the room in a hurry. Vidia let out her breath with a sigh of relief. But the good feeling didn't last long. Because following close on Lizzy's heels was *the cat*.

Vidia flew from window to window until she found herself looking in on the upstairs landing. She saw Lizzy arrive at the top of the stairs carrying the fairy house. The cat slunk along right behind her.

The little girl turned and disappeared into one of the bedrooms. Again Vidia zipped around the corner of the house, peering into windows until she found Lizzy's bedroom.

Vidia watched Lizzy put the fairy house down and look inside. She looked in one window, then another, as if trying to find Tinker Bell. "Where have you gone?" she said aloud.

Hmmmm, Vidia wondered. Where was Tink? Had she somehow managed to escape?

Clearly, Lizzy was wondering the same thing. And as Vidia watched, Lizzy lifted off the entire roof of the house so she could look down inside it.

She reeled back when Tinker Bell came rocketing out.

Tinker Bell shot up so fast, she smacked right into the canopy of the bed and fell back down on the blanket, dazed.

The cat pounced on the bed. Tink jumped up and made

a run for it, diving under a pillow. The cat dove under the pillow, too, and Tinker Bell ran out the other side.

Before he could snatch her, Lizzy grabbed Tinker Bell and swooped her out of harm's way. She quickly stuffed Tink into a birdcage and yelled at the cat. "Mr. Twitches. *No!* Out! Out! Bad cat. No! No! No!"

Lizzy turned back to the cage. "Don't worry, little fairy. Mr. Twitches won't bother you as long as you're in there." She grabbed the cat and went to the door. "Naughty cat. You're going downstairs."

As Lizzy left the room with Mr. Twitches, Vidia struggled to open the window, without success.

Inside the birdcage, Tinker Bell was really worried now, red-faced and puffing. The latch was firmly locked from the outside. The door wouldn't budge.

Vidia realized there was no way she could rescue Tinker Bell on her own. She would have to go back to the camp for help. She looked up at the sky with a worried frown.

Dark clouds were gathering. That meant rain. Rain meant wet wings. And wet wings meant she might have to find her way back to camp on foot.

Vidia spread her wings and took to the sky.

She had to hurry. Tinker Bell's life depended on it.

Vidia flew as hard and as fast as she could, but she couldn't beat the storm. Thunder rumbled and lightning flashed. She was just reaching the open meadow when the rain came pouring down in sheets.

A raindrop the size of a strawberry fell right on top of her, exploding against her back and wings. Then another raindrop exploded on her head. The weight of Vidia's wet wings pulled her to the ground. She had no choice but to walk.

Finally, after what seemed like hours, Vidia stumbled into the fairy camp, drenched and exhausted. She spotted

Iridessa, Rosetta, Silvermist, Clank, and Bobble waiting for the rain to stop under the canopy of a leafy bush.

"Tinker Bell's been captured by humans!" shouted Vidia, stumbling toward them.

Clank's face registered his alarm. "What's this? Tinker Bell?"

"In trouble?" Bobble jumped to his feet.

"Where is she?" Iridessa demanded

"What happened?" Rosetta gasped.

"Tinker Bell went into this little house in the meadow and couldn't get back out. The door was jammed. Then this human came from out of nowhere and snatched her up." Vidia went on, "I know where she is. We have to hurry and save her."

Fawn frowned, looking out over the landscape. "We can't fly in the rain. And the meadow's already flooded."

"Maybe we don't have to fly," Clank said. His eyes grew wide and he suddenly seemed very excited. "If we get some big leaves and sew them together with stem twine . . ."

Bobble caught on immediately. "Aye, and miter-cut some twigs for the subflooring . . ."

Clank looked downright giddy now. "Oh, and we can hold it all together with some two-and-a-quarter mooring vines."

"What are you two talking about?" demanded Vidia. Honestly! Had they forgotten that this was an emergency?

Clank threw her a puzzled look, as if he couldn't believe she hadn't caught on already. It was so obvious!

"We're going to build a boat," Clank and Bobble answered in unison.

Seven

Vidia watched as the crew worked on the boat as a team, united in their purpose and determined to rescue their friend Tinker Bell. It was all Tink's own fault, but still, if Vidia hadn't tried to play that trick with the door . . .

Vidia blocked her train of thought. No time for that now. She watched Fawn, Silvermist, and a group of pill bugs drape a lily pad over the deck of the boat to form a canopy.

It was such a long shot, and yet everyone worked with such fierce determination. Vidia couldn't help wondering—if she were the one in trouble and not Tinker Bell, would they be working this hard to save her?

She had the uneasy feeling that the answer might be

no. So she decided to block that train of thought, too. Right now, what was important was getting Tinker Bell back.

Vidia secured a mooring line, her face skeptical. "This thing had better work," she muttered.

Rosetta took one of the mushroom caps and positioned it so that it functioned as a bumper, while Blaze flew in with a line and tied it in place.

Pill bugs bounced up and down like jumping beans, hammering nuts and bolts into place.

"More reeds over here!" Clank shouted.

Clank, Bobble, and a swarm of bees worked together to make a sail.

Bobble sewed the sail with a large needle and thread. Haste made him careless, and he poked his hand with every stitch. "Ow! Ow! Ow!" he chanted as the sewing continued.

Clank supervised all the work. He called out encouragement to the fairies, along with directions, in his big, gruff voice. "Come on . . . come on . . . Let's get going."

Bobble hurried from one task to the next, urging everyone on. "There you go. Now you're talking."

Finally, Cheese tugged a rope and raised the mast. "It's working!" Clank shouted happily.

The boat was complete. Soon they would set sail and rescue Tinker Bell. Vidia stared out at the fairy camp with worried eyes. It was practically a swamp. Torrential rain had soaked everybody and everything. This was going to be a dangerous journey.

One by one, the fairies boarded the boat. Finally, they all stood huddled in the bow, ready to cast off.

"Well." Silvermist gulped. "This is it."

Fawn stuck her hand out. "Hey, faith . . ."

Iridessa put her hand on top of Fawn's. ". . . trust . . . ," she said.

Rosetta and Silvermist put their hands on top of the others and recited the rest of the pledge together, like a team in a huddle. ". . . and pixie dust."

Vidia stood slightly apart. She wasn't what you would call a team player—but she was just as determined to save Tinker Bell as the others.

Meanwhile, Tinker Bell stood in the birdcage examining the lock, trying to open it. "Come on. Come *on,*" she muttered furiously.

Suddenly, she heard the door open. The little human girl was back.

Tinker Bell backed up and sank down in the center of the birdcage.

"You don't have to be scared," the little girl told her. "I'm very nice."

Tinker Bell turned her head away. Nice little girls didn't trap fairies in cages.

Outside, the storm raged and thundered. Tinker Bell

had never been so scared. Lizzy stared at her through the bars. "You're so little," she said. "Your dress is very leafy. Did you make it yourself? I like your wings. They're like sparkly lace. Your hair must be so soft, like silk.

"Are you hungry?" the little girl asked then. She gingerly poked a piece of crumpet through the bars of the cage.

Tinker Bell backed away from it. She didn't want anything to do with this human or her food.

"Maybe not. That's okay," said Lizzy. "I don't like some kinds of food, either."

She noticed the spring from the lock lying on the bottom of the cage and realized that Tinker Bell had been trying to get out. "Oh! So sorry! Where are my manners?" Lizzy quickly opened the door of the cage.

Tink grabbed her chance and darted toward the window, but she couldn't open it.

Lizzy came running toward her and Tinker Bell flew as far away from her as she could, zipping up into the rafters and hovering as close to the ceiling as she could get.

Lizzy looked up. “Don’t be afraid. You’re safe here.” She backed off, seeming to realize that chasing Tinker Bell around the room wasn’t the best way to reassure her. “I just want to be friends. Look. I’ve been drawing fairies all my life.” Lizzy gestured toward her desk and the wall.

Tinker Bell followed the sweep of Lizzy’s arm with her eyes. *Wow!* The room was a treasure trove of fairy art and artifacts. Tacked to the wall were lovely paintings and engravings of fairies. Fairies dancing. Fairies flying. Fairies reclining on toadstools.

Next to the paintings and engravings, Lizzy had hung her own drawings and paintings. They weren’t professional like the others, but they were expressive. And her love for fairies was clear in every stroke of her pen and brush.

Tinker Bell couldn’t help flying down to get a closer look.

“I just love fairies,” Lizzy said. “I know all about you,

too. There are lots of different kinds of fairies."

Lizzy held up a couple of drawings that had been lying on her worktable. One depicted a fairy talking to a chipmunk. The other showed a fairy sitting on a flower.

"Some of you can talk to animals," Lizzy continued. "And some of you can make flowers bloom. And there are even fairies that color the rainbow."

Now that Tinker Bell had gotten over her fear, she was fascinated by this little girl. Lizzy seemed to know so much about fairies. How could this be? She was right about every detail.

Lizzy held up another picture. "This is a water fairy. You can tell because her skin is blue."

Blue? Okay. Clearly Lizzy wasn't fully informed. Tinker Bell had met every single water fairy, and not one of them was blue.

"And this is a candy fairy," Lizzy said. "She's sitting in a lollipop tree and . . ."

Tinker Bell shook her head again. Candy fairies? Lollipop trees? Where was Lizzy getting this nonsense?

"You live under rocks and stones, and you make furniture out of potatoes. A fairy circle is a ring of mushrooms," Lizzy continued happily, "and if a person steps in it, a fairy has to grant them three wishes from their magic bag. But if they don't, they turn into a pile of delicious sugar, and then . . ."

Tink couldn't take it anymore. The poor kid was so confused. Tink flew a little closer. "Wait a minute! Where are you getting all this?" she asked.

But all Lizzy heard was a pretty ringing sound. Her mouth curved into a wide smile. "You jingle when you talk! Like a little bell. So *that's* how fairies speak."

Tinker Bell frowned. Was that what this little girl heard? Not words, but jingling?

"Do all fairies sound the same when they talk?"

Before Tinker Bell could even think how to respond, the little girl began peppering her with questions. "So what do you think of my fairies? Oh! And my fairy house? It got a little shaken up." She retrieved the two pieces of the fairy house from the floor and placed them together on the desk.

Tinker Bell pointed. "Did you make that?"

Lizzy cocked her head as if she was trying to decode the jingling sound she heard. "I don't know what you're saying."

Tinker Bell sighed. As much as Lizzy seemed to connect with fairies, it was clear she couldn't hear their language. But there were other ways to communicate. Tinker Bell pantomimed using a hammer and then a saw.

Lizzy understood. "Oh! You want to know if I made the fairy house. Yes, I did. Do you like it?"

Tinker Bell nodded enthusiastically. She took another look at the house and pointed to the door. She wanted to make Lizzy understand that the door was stuck. Tinker Bell pulled at the door handle, but it wouldn't open.

"Oh! The door is stuck?"

"Yeah, bit of a problem for me earlier," Tinker Bell said dryly, even though she knew her tone would be lost in jingling translation.

She decided to show Lizzy that the two of them had a few things in common—like a knack for fixing things.

Eight

Tinker Bell made a "watch this" motion. Then she strode up to the door and went to work.

Using her hip and shoulder, she gave the door a knock here and a tug there. Then she tightened the hinges with a deft twist.

She opened the door with a flourish. "Ta-da!"

Lizzy's mouth fell open in astonishment. "You're quite the little tinker, aren't you?"

Tinker Bell pointed to her nose and gestured toward herself, inviting Lizzy to guess her name.

"What? Is that your name? Tinker?"

Tinker Bell nodded, then reached into the house and tapped the little bell hanging next to the door.

"Uh . . . bell. Oh! Your name is Bell?"

Tinker Bell continued the pantomime, coaching Lizzy along. She hammered and sawed and then rang the bell again.

"Tinker . . . Bell . . ."

Tinker Bell held out her hands and then slowly moved them together.

"Tinker Bell?" Lizzy guessed.

Tinker Bell flew into the air and struck a pose that clearly said, "That's me!"

"Tinker Bell," Lizzy breathed. "What a lovely name. Well, Tinker Bell, my name is Lizzy Griffiths." The little girl's voice was full of delight that she and Tinker Bell were now communicating.

At that moment, Lizzy and Tink both heard a footstep outside the door.

"Lizzy?" a voice called. It was the little girl's father!

As the door opened, Lizzy motioned to Tinker Bell to

hide behind one of her fairy figurines.

"Who are you talking to?" the father asked.

"Oh, um . . ." Lizzy quickly held up one of her drawings. "My fairy! I'm just pretending, Father."

"That's nice, dear. I brought you something I think you'll really enjoy. These are some of my old field journals. I picked out the ones I thought would excite you the most."

He dropped a big stack of journals on Lizzy's table and selected one to show her. "This one on rocks and minerals is particularly interesting."

Lizzy made a face that Tink could see but her father couldn't. Finally she asked, "Is there a field journal about fairies?"

Dr. Griffiths laughed. "Of course not, Lizzy. Books like this are based on fact and scientific research." He wandered over toward Lizzy's collection of fairy figurines. Tinker Bell tried her best to stay still when he reached down and picked up the one right in front of her. "Which is quite the contrary of your little figurines and drawings, which—although lovely—are completely fictitious."

Lizzy reached out to take the figurine from her father and tried not to look at Tinker Bell. "Oh, I'll take that, Father."

He handed her a large notebook. "Here is a blank field journal." He smiled fondly. "You're very talented, my darling. I'm sure you'll be able to fill it with your own scientific research."

Lizzy took the journal. "Yes, Father."

Their conversation was interrupted by the loud sound of *drip . . . drip . . . drip*—coming from outside the bedroom.

Dr. Griffiths peered toward the hall, where the rain was leaking in. Shaking his head in frustration, he went into the hallway to collect his tools and buckets. "Now, if only those leaks were just pretend," he joked.

As soon as he closed the door behind him, Lizzy called to Tinker Bell. "You can come out now."

Tink pointed toward the window. "I really should be—"

Lizzy understood. "You want to go?"

Tinker Bell nodded and Lizzy sadly walked to the window and opened it. Tinker bell noticed the pouring rain, and her shoulders slumped. Flying through that would be impossible. To go on foot would be too dangerous.

"What's wrong?" Lizzy asked. "Can't you fly in the rain?"

Tinker Bell shook her head.

"You can stay with me until the rain stops," Lizzy said brightly. "Then you can teach me more about fairies."

Tinker Bell cast her eye out the window. There was no way she could fly all the way back to camp in this storm. What would be the harm in spending a little more time with Lizzy? "Well," Tinker Bell joked, "the only way I could get back to fairy camp now is if I had a boat."

The fairy rescue party was fighting its way through turbulent waters as they floated within a wheel rut carved out in a dirt road.

Bobble was trying to be optimistic. "We're almost there. Why, look, we're picking up speed already."

"Did you hear that?" Iridessa said happily. "We're moving faster."

Fawn, however, still looked dubious. Without a word, she climbed the mast so she could see what was up ahead.

"Hey, guys!" Fawn shouted. "We're heading right for a waterfall!"

Clank, now a bit seasick, called out instructions. "Loosen the ropes and . . . *Urp!*" He belched softly. "Turn the sail."

Vidia and Rosetta both ran to the same rope. "I got it," Vidia snapped.

"Hey!" Rosetta protested.

Meanwhile, Iridessa was working on another rope,

muttering the instructions to herself. "Back and down around the loop and up and through." The rope loosened. "I did it!" Iridessa cried happily. But before she even had a chance to smile, the rope slipped out of her hand and the sail went spinning out of control with Fawn still hanging on to it.

"Turn the boat!" Vidia yelled. *"Turn the boat!"* She ran to the back of the boat and grabbed the rudder away from Silvermist. "Here, let me. I can do it . . . I can . . ." Vidia gave the rudder a yank, and *snap!* It broke off in her hand.

"Guuuuuys!" Fawn shouted from the top of the sail. "We're running out of river."

Silvermist stepped heroically forward. "That's all right," she said in a dramatic tone. "Because all we need is a *little*! Rosetta, come grab my feet." Silvermist moved quickly to the front of the boat, which began tipping over the falls. She fell forward just as Rosetta grabbed her ankles, keeping her from plunging in headfirst.

"Hang on," Bobble moaned. "We're going straight down."

"Brace yourselves," Rosetta said, tightening her grip on Silvermist's ankles.

Vidia and the others grabbed the sides of the boat as it began plummeting downward.

Silvermist calmly closed her eyes and dangled her fingertips in the water. Using all her water-fairy magic and strength, she turned the waterfall into a bridge.

The fairies felt a surge beneath them as the boat rose. Amazing! Even Vidia felt a grudging admiration. She'd never had much use for other fairy talents before, but this was pretty impressive.

It was a wild ride. They all hunkered down as the boat careened across the water bridge like an out-of-control surfboard.

Vidia closed her eyes and felt herself tumble through the air before landing—*splat!*—in a big pile of weeds.

Smack!

Thud!

Bam!

She heard the others landing on the ground around her like wet fish.

Nine

Tinker Bell flew over to a beautiful Victorian dollhouse in the corner of Lizzy's room.

"This is my dollhouse," Lizzy explained. "Do you have a house, too?"

Tinker Bell nodded.

"Is it like this one?"

"Well . . ."

"What color is it? Is it far from here? Through the forest? Is it in Fairyland?" Lizzy finally took a breath. "Oh, tell me you live in Fairyland!"

Tinker Bell couldn't help laughing. "Hold on! Hold on!" She flew to the shelf and picked up a jar of art supplies, bringing it back to the worktable. "Let's do this right," she said. She put down the art supplies and opened the blank field journal. She gestured toward the blank page.

Lizzy immediately understood what Tinker Bell was proposing. "Perfect!" She threw herself into a chair and picked up her very best pen. Working carefully, Lizzy wrote SCIENTIFIC FAIRY RESEARCH on the title page. "Okay. What's your favorite color?" she asked Tinker Bell.

Tinker Bell pointed to her green dress. Lizzy's mouth dropped open in surprise. "Green is my favorite color, too!" She began to write it down, then stopped. "Oh! I should start from the beginning. Where do fairies come from? I mean, where were you born?"

"Oh! Well. Hmmm. That one's a little more complicated, because . . ." Tinker Bell began again. "So a baby, when it laughs for the first time . . ." Tinker Bell stopped. She was going to need props.

She flew over to the shelf and returned with a baby doll. She rocked it in her arms and looked lovingly down at it. Then she gently wiggled the baby doll in her arms and pretended to laugh.

"You were a funny-looking baby?" Lizzy guessed.

Tink's huge smile turned to a frown. No. *Think! Think!* She told herself. What was another way to get at it? She held the baby doll out and prompted Lizzy to guess what she was trying to say.

"A baby," Lizzy said.

Tink mimed laughing.

"Laughs," Lizzy continued.

Tink held up one index finger.

"One," Lizzy said.

Tinker Bell waved her hands and held up the index finger one more time.

"First?" Lizzy tried tentatively.

Tink nodded emphatically.

"When a baby laughs for the first time, that's when a fairy is born?" Lizzy ventured.

Tinker Bell nodded again and smiled happily. *Wow!* This little girl was smart.

"Incredible," Lizzy said softly.

"Lizzy, that's only the beginning." Tinker Bell picked up scissors and a piece of green construction paper. There was so much to tell. So much for Lizzy to learn.

The next two hours went speeding by for both Lizzy and Tinker Bell. The scientific fairy research project forced both of them to be imaginative and creative.

Tinker Bell cut out grass from the green paper and raised it from behind the table to show that it was growing. Lizzy understood and wrote, "Helps the grass grow," beside her entry on garden fairies.

Tinker Bell pretended to take a toothpick out of a teddy bear's paw, and Lizzy wrote, "Animal fairies help injured animals." Then, with Tinker Bell's help, she drew a picture of Fawn.

Tink showed Lizzy what fairies ate by making a "yummy

yummy" face at a berry and a peanut, and a "yucky yucky" face at a gnat. Lizzy smiled and wrote, "Not carnivores."

Lizzy sketched a picture of Tinker Bell riding a unicorn, but Tinker Bell shook her head. Tinker Bell realized she was a little like Dr. Griffiths. No point in stuffing the child's head with fictitious nonsense. Lizzy needed to fill her field guide with the facts and nothing but the facts.

Tinker Bell guided Lizzy's crayon so that Silvermist's dress—but not her skin—was blue. She drew the stars on a blackboard and taught Lizzy how to spot the Second Star to the Right. She taught Lizzy about fairies' natural enemies by making a shadow picture of a hawk.

Last but not least, she lay on the page while Lizzy traced around her and labeled the drawing ACTUAL SIZE.

Tink was very pleased with the drawing. It only needed one small touch to finish it off. She took two little pieces of cotton balls and glued them to the tips of her shoes in the drawing.

When the field journal was almost finished, Tinker Bell turned it back to the page on animal fairies. She quickly added a paintbrush in the hand of one of the animal fairies depicted on the page. And then Tink sketched the outline of a butterfly with no markings. The butterfly hovered like a blank canvas waiting to be painted.

"I knew it!" Lizzy cried. "I knew it. I knew it! I knew it!" She was so excited to discover that her theory about butterflies was correct that she bounced up and down in her chair, making a tremendous happy racket.

"I told Father that fairies painted butterfly wings, but he didn't believe me! Well, I'll bet he believes me now that it's official scientific research!"

Lizzy flipped through the journal they had created. "I can't believe how many different types of fairies there are!"

Tinker Bell fluttered over the journal and admired each page. All of Tinker Bell's friends were there. Fawn. Silvermist. Iridessa. Rosetta. And Terence.

Tinker Bell is very curious about human things.

Vidia reminds Tink that fairies aren't supposed to go near humans.

Tinker Bell finds a house built for fairies!

Tinker Bell goes inside the house.

Vidia gets mad at Tink and uses
her fairy magic to slam the door shut!

The house was built by a little girl named Lizzy.
She is so excited to have caught a real fairy!

Tinker Bell's friends are looking for her.

With Tinker Bell and the other fairies by her side, Lizzy is ready for her first outdoor flight.

Vidia gets stuck in the mud, and Iridessa is worried.

Tinker Bell and Lizzy become best friends,
and Tink teaches Lizzy to fly!

Sadness welled up in Tink's heart. Lizzy seemed to sense it. "Who are they?" she asked softly.

Tink pantomimed holding something close to her heart.

"They're your friends? I bet they miss you." Tinker Bell knew Lizzy was right. She just hoped she could see her friends again soon.

Ten

"Who's alive?" Silvermist asked. All around them, the boat lay in pieces.

"Not me," Iridessa groaned.

Clank sat up and took his own pulse. "I am."

Fawn stared at her foot, which was bent completely backward. *"Argh!"* she groaned. She touched it again, trying to twist it into the right position.

"Argh!" Rosetta echoed, lifting her head and glowering at Fawn.

Fawn let go of the foot, realizing it was Rosetta's and not hers. "Sorry."

The group slowly pulled themselves together, standing up and brushing debris and mud from their clothes. They shook their heads and stared at what was left of their boat.

"Looks like we're walking from here," Vidia said.

"But walking where?" asked Fawn.

"We could be anywhere," Iridessa pointed out.

The fairies looked around. They were in some kind of valley, with grass towering over them on all sides.

Bobble grabbed a leaf and held it over his head like an umbrella. "Everything looks the same from down here."

Clank was equally flummoxed. "And there's no way of knowing which way to go." He picked something up off the ground and sheltered himself with it. Whatever it was, it wasn't much larger in diameter than his own head.

Vidia stared at Clank, unable to believe what she was seeing. She pointed at his makeshift rain hat. "Clank! Where did you find that?" she demanded.

"Here on the ground. Is it yours?" He held it out to her, but Vidia walked past him with her eyes glued to the ground.

The makeshift rain hat was a button! And Vidia was looking for more of them. There they were! There . . . there . . . and there.

Vidia turned to the others, her face triumphant. "I know where we are!" She lowered her head and beckoned to the rest of the fairies to follow. She hoped she was going the right way and not betraying their trust—the way she'd betrayed Tinker Bell.

"Tinker Bell, this is so fascinating." Tinker Bell and Lizzy were hard at work, putting the finishing touches on Lizzy's fairy field journal.

Tink handed Lizzy the scissors. "Thank you," Lizzy said as she began cutting out more fairies while Tinker Bell used a crayon to draw a snowflake.

Lizzy brushed a bit of paste on a page, placed a cutout

fairy over it, and pressed. "Well, I think we've covered everything. I hope Father's impressed."

She held up the journal and admired it. "Types of fairies. Their talents. And now, for the finale." Lizzy opened a page, and up popped a three-dimensional display of Pixie Hollow. "It worked!" she said happily.

Tinker Bell floated around the journal, applauding.

"Oh, Tinker Bell. I can't wait to show Father."

Tinker Bell gestured to Lizzy and pointed toward the door. "Then go now!"

Lizzy smiled brightly. "It's time. Let me just do one more thing." She picked up a crayon and wrote in big, neat letters on the front of the journal: ELIZABETH GRIFFITHS AND . . . Lizzy handed the crayon to Tinker Bell.

Touched and happy, Tinker Bell took the crayon and wrote her name on the cover, too. TINKER BELL.

Tinker Bell was proud of the book they had created. It had been fun, but she still missed her friends.

Lizzy saw the expression on Tink's face and knew what she should do. She walked over to the window. "It looks like the rain has let up some," she said. "You might be able to make it home to your friends now."

In her heart, Lizzy wanted Tinker Bell to stay, but she also understood how important the other fairies were to Tink. Lizzy wanted to help out her new friend.

It was still drizzling, so Lizzy handed Tinker Bell one of the paper hats they had made. "Maybe this could help you." Tinker Bell looked at the hat and smiled. She flew over to the table, where she picked up a paintbrush and brought it back to Lizzy. Always the inventive tinker fairy, Tink poked the paintbrush through the paper hat, making a fairy-sized umbrella.

Lizzy was sad to see Tink go. "Take care of yourself," she said, sniffling to hold back her tears. "I'll never forget you, Tinker Bell."

Tink headed out the window, but she turned back for a

last look just as Lizzy was picking up the fairy journal to take it to her father. "I'll never forget you, Lizzy," Tinker Bell said softly.

Eleven

The rain had let up a bit, but everything was still wet. In the distance, Tink could see the oak tree where the fairy camp was. She knew it was time to leave.

Tinker Bell's heart sank as she realized that on her very first day, she had gotten herself captured, and had probably caused a lot of worry back at fairy camp.

She flew down from the window, keeping a sharp eye out for the cat. When she flew past Dr. Griffiths's study, she paused to look in, hoping to see father and daughter united over Lizzy's project.

But as she hovered, she heard voices through the partly opened window.

"Father, look!"

"Not just now, Lizzy."

Tinker Bell fluttered to the window to investigate. It was quite a scene. The ceiling was leaking in several places, and strewn around the room were buckets, pots, and pans to catch the water. Dr. Griffiths was busy trying to stop one of the leaks in the ceiling.

Lizzy held out her journal. "I made it especially for you, Father. It's just like your field journal. It's filled with lots of facts."

Dr. Griffiths climbed up on his desk and mopped at the wet ceiling with a cloth. He was clearly flustered and frustrated.

"Yes, yes, Lizzy. That sounds wonderful. But I'm in the middle of a potential catastrophe here. I can't look at it now."

"But, Father. It's a field journal, and I—"

"I don't have time," Dr. Griffiths insisted in an exasperated voice, trying to stuff a little piece of cloth into a crack in the ceiling. "I have to stop these leaks before it starts pouring."

The cloth seemed to stop the flow of drips for a moment. "There we go," Dr. Griffiths said with a sigh.

"That's not how you fix it," Tinker Bell muttered under her breath.

A drop of water came through the cloth and fell on Dr. Griffiths.

"Told you," Tink muttered again.

Dr. Griffiths jumped off the desk and began to move his paperwork away from the dripping water.

"When will you be able to look at it?" Lizzy asked him.

"I don't know," her father sighed. "Maybe later."

Lizzy turned away and hugged the journal against her chest. "You always say that," she said in a glum tone. Tinker Bell watched her leave the room, unnoticed by Dr. Griffiths.

Torn, Tinker Bell looked back toward the tall oak tree.

Her friends would be worried about her. She wanted to go back. She *needed* to go back. But she also knew Lizzy would be feeling pretty lonely. Tink had a big choice to make.

Tinker Bell flew back into Lizzy's room, approaching slowly so she wouldn't startle her.

Lizzy gasped. *"Tinker Bell!"* she cried in a joyous voice. "You came back!"

Tinker Bell floated down onto her hand. "I couldn't leave my friend," she said.

Lizzy smiled. She might not have understood Tink's words, but she heard the warm offer of friendship, clear as a bell. "I'm so glad to see you," she said. "Father has no time for the field journal."

Tink flew up and lifted Lizzy's chin, wiping the tears away. "I think I can fix that," she jingled.

Twelve

"Vidia," Rosetta said, "are you sure you know where you're going?"

"Yes. Tinker Bell and I walked by here. I just have to find the road."

Fawn fell into step on the other side of Vidia. "Road? What road?"

Vidia reached forward and parted some tall grass. "That road."

"That's not a road anymore," Iridessa protested. "That's a muddy river."

"So I guess we need to find a bridge," Rosetta suggested.

But Vidia didn't want to risk taking a detour and getting lost. Tink needed them right away. She drew a deep breath and jumped, landing in the muddy water up to her knees.

"Or," Rosetta added, "we could be spontaneous and jump right in."

"It's not deep," Vidia pointed out. "We could walk across."

Fawn jumped in, and then Iridessa and Silvermist. Bobble and Clank plowed in, making major splashes. Only Rosetta hesitated on the bank. "I don't really do mud," she explained.

"But . . . you're a *garden fairy,*" Vidia pointed out.

Rosetta gave her an embarrassed smile. "Ironic, isn't it?"

"Rosetta!" the fairies all shouted.

"Okay. All right. I'm coming." Rosetta took off her sandals and stepped daintily into the water. "*Ewwww!* Ooooh. What was that?"

Vidia rolled her eyes and waved her arms like a crossing guard, urging Rosetta across. One by one, Vidia watched all the fairies cross safely and climb up the bank. Once everyone was on the other side, Vidia followed. She took a step and . . . sank waist deep into a sucking pool of mud. Vidia gritted her teeth and struggled, trying to wrench herself loose.

"She's stuck," Clank said, pointing out the obvious.

Vidia gave it one last try, but it was no use. "All right, all right. Someone just get me something to grab on to."

"Got it!" Bobble said. "Clanky: rescue device!" Clank and Bobble hurried into the weeds in search of something to pull Vidia out with.

Rosetta, Iridessa, and Fawn climbed back into the mud and waded to Vidia's side. Each one of them grabbed an arm. "Okay," Fawn said, "let's give this a try. Pull!"

The girls gave Vidia a tremendous yank. Vidia felt a definite tremble in the mud.

"Do you feel that?" Iridessa. "She's starting to break free."

"I don't think so," Silvermist said in a wary tone.

Then they heard it. A noise. Loud and angry. The sound of an engine.

The girls looked up and saw a flash of light.

"It's an angry human machine!" cried Silvermist as they all noticed the oncoming car.

The girls began to tug and tug, desperate to free Vidia before the machine ran them over. Only Iridessa did nothing. She stood perfectly still.

"Light!" whispered Iridessa, as if mesmerized.

The car came around the bend. The full glare of the headlights played over the road. Iridessa began walking straight toward the oncoming machine. The headlights illuminated her in a blaze. At that very moment, she lifted her hand.

Vidia and the others gasped. Using all her strength and her light-fairy magic, Iridessa cupped her hand and bent the beam of light backward, sending it straight at the oncoming driver. From his perspective, it looked as if a motorcycle's headlight had suddenly appeared in the road.

The driver slammed on his brakes. The automobile careened toward Vidia and her protectors. They huddled together, watching with huge frightened eyes.

The automobile veered wildly to the side and skidded to a stop at the last possible second.

The door opened and they saw a huge boot step out.

Vidia's heart thundered in her chest. The automobile hadn't run over them, but they were still far from safe. She was still stuck, and a human with very large feet was stomping around in the dark.

"Hello!" the human shouted. "Is somebody out there? Anybody? Hello?"

The big boots came closer.

Vidia felt Fawn poking her. Why? What was she trying to tell her?

Fawn pointed to the human's untied bootlace. It lay on

the ground inches away. Fawn picked it up. "Grab this!" she hissed. "Hurry!"

"Are you kidding me?" Vidia asked.

"Trust me," Fawn urged. "And hold on tight."

Every fairy grabbed the bootlace, including Vidia.

"Hello?" the driver called out one last time. "Anybody?"

When no one answered, he turned, and as he picked up his giant foot . . . *plop!* Vidia came up out of the mud, along with everybody else.

The human swung his foot forward, toward the car. The girls let go and dropped safely to the ground at the side of the road. They scrambled out of the way as the driver climbed back into the automobile, started up the engine, and roared off.

They watched the lights disappear around the bend. Usually, an escape this close and this clever would have been the cause of much celebration. But everyone was quiet and somber.

They still had a job to do. They had to find Tinker Bell and rescue her.

Vidia was grateful for the help, but she also felt guilty. They had all come so close to being killed. And it was all her fault. Why had she always thought Tinker Bell was the troublemaker? Why had she taken so much pride in having no friends?

Vidia shook herself, swallowed the lump in her throat, and gestured to the group to keep moving.

Thirteen

Lizzy was tired. Tinker Bell sat beside her on her pillow and waited for the little girl to fall asleep. Tink looked around the room and smiled.

It was a mess, but a lovely sort of mess. The kind of mess that happened when two good friends got together to play.

They each held an empty teacup, and Lizzy was sleepily instructing Tink in tea party etiquette. "You hold your pinky out, like this," she said, fighting a yawn. "And that's the way"—her eyelids fluttered heavily—"you throw a proper tea party," she finished, her voice little more than a murmur as she fell into slumber.

Tinker Bell waited a moment to be sure she was sound

asleep, then gently pulled the covers up and tucked her in. "Good night, Lizzy," she said quietly, knowing that if Lizzy heard anything at all, it would be nothing but a quiet jingle.

Tinker Bell heard footsteps on the creaking stairs.

She was scared for a second, but it wasn't the cat—it was Dr. Griffiths.

He stepped silently into the room and stood beside the bed. Tinker Bell watched his face soften as he looked down on his little girl. He gently adjusted the covers and shook his head regretfully. "There just aren't enough hours in the day," he muttered.

Tinker Bell quietly followed him out of the room. This father and daughter clearly loved each other, but somehow, they couldn't seem to spend time together.

Tink was happy to see that Lizzy's father felt this way. Originally, she thought he was a mean person, but now she saw he cared. There was just too much to do!

Out in the hallway, Dr. Griffiths stopped and looked up.

Tinker Bell followed his gaze. *Oops!* She'd forgotten about the leak in the ceiling.

Tools lay on the floor. It was clear to Tinker Bell that Dr. Griffiths had been working—unsuccessfully—to fix the leak.

Dr. Griffiths shook his head in a gesture of defeat. "I'm going to bed," he muttered. He placed a bucket underneath the leak. Then he headed down the hallway toward his own room.

When Dr. Griffiths closed his door, Tinker Bell flew down to his office and saw more buckets and more leaks. She flew closer to the ceiling and found a small hole leading into the dusty attic.

Tinker Bell flew about the attic gathering supplies. She snatched up some rope, old tubing, a funnel, and a copper connector shaped like a *T*. Tink knew just what to do.

She cut some of the tubing, fastened it to the copper connector, rigged the rope, tied the funnel, and, with a few deft twists of the tubing, redirected all the leaking water through an open vent, where it poured harmlessly outside into a flower bed. It had taken most of the night, but her mission had been accomplished.

Or had it?

She knew how important it was to double-check her work.

Tinker Bell zipped down to Dr. Griffiths's office to make sure the leaks had stopped. When she got there, she felt the happy tingle of a job well done. Not a leak in sight.

A movement on Dr. Griffiths's desk caught her attention. It was the butterfly—still trapped in a jar!

Tinker Bell's work wasn't finished after all. There was one more little thing she needed to do.

When morning came, Tinker Bell flew to Lizzy. She tugged at the little girl's nightgown until she awoke.

Lizzy opened her eyes and smiled. "Good morning, Tinker Bell. How did you sleep?"

"Well, actually, I didn't. But that doesn't matter. You should go downstairs to your father."

As Lizzy tried to understand Tink, there was a brisk knock on the bedroom door. "Lizzy?" Dr. Griffiths opened the door.

Tinker Bell dove behind a pile of stuffed animals.

"Yes, Father?"

"Good morning, my dear. All the leaks seem to have stopped. I just wanted to make sure everything is okay in here."

"Oh, yes. Just fine. No leaks at all."

"Strange," Dr. Griffiths commented. "It's as if the leaks mended themselves."

Lizzy threw an inquiring look in Tink's direction. Tinker Bell winked to say, "Yep! It was me."

Dr. Griffiths frowned. "It's still raining outside. I can't

imagine how on earth such a thing could occur."

Tinker Bell motioned to Lizzy to go with her father. But Lizzy didn't seem to get it. She smiled at her father and impatiently shifted her weight from one foot to the other.

"Well, there must be an explanation that I'm just not thinking of," Dr. Griffiths continued.

Lizzy began to gently shepherd her father toward the door. "Well, I'm sure you'll think of it, Father. Perhaps down in your office! You always do your best thinking there. I wish you luck!"

Dr. Griffiths seemed to take the hint and did his best to smile brightly. "Oh, off we go . . ." He paused a moment and looked at Lizzy, clearly hoping she might suggest that they spend the morning together. Tink wondered why he didn't suggest it himself; then she realized that Dr. Griffiths was actually shy around his daughter. After another moment, he made a vague wave and left the room.

Lizzy closed the door. "Whew! That was close."

Tinker Bell was frustrated. *Good grief!* Like father, like daughter. Couldn't Lizzy see that her father wanted to spend time with her?

She flew toward Lizzy and held out her hands. "What are you doing?" she said. "This is your chance."

Lizzy looked confused.

Now Tinker Bell was losing her patience. She flew over to the fairy field journal, picked it up, and held it out to Lizzy.

Lizzy thought for a moment, then finally understood. "Is that why you fixed those leaks? So he can spend more time with me?"

Tinker Bell nodded.

Lizzy took the field journal. "I've really been wanting to show him this. He has so much to learn about fairies."

Tinker Bell gestured vigorously toward the door, and Lizzy giggled at her. "Okay. Okay. I'll go."

Lizzy hurried from the room. Tinker Bell followed at a

discreet distance. She watched Lizzy bound down the stairs and hover in the doorway of her father's study. "Father, since you have more time, maybe I can show you my field journal. . . ."

But when Dr. Griffiths spoke, his voice was distraught. "The butterfly is gone."

"What?" Lizzy cried.

Tinker Bell put a hand to her mouth.

Dr. Griffiths walked into the hallway with the empty jar in his hand. Tinker Bell backed out of sight.

"The *Apatura iris* with the irregular wing pattern. I was going to present it to the museum this evening. Now it's gone. Elizabeth, did you release it?"

"No," Lizzy answered.

Dr. Griffiths's face was angry. "Well, I didn't do it. And since there is no one else in the house, there is only one logical explanation. It must have been you."

"I didn't do it, Father."

Dr. Griffiths glowered. “I’m going to give you one more chance. Tell me the truth!”

“I could tell you.” Lizzy’s voice grew defiant. “But you wouldn’t believe me.”

“Very well—off to your room, young lady. I’m very disappointed in you.”

From her hiding place behind Lizzy’s nightgown, Tinker Bell fluttered sadly. All her efforts had backfired. She had driven Lizzy and her father even further apart.

Fourteen

Vidia led the rescue party across the grassy field toward the house. The closer the group got to their destination, the quieter they became. It was as if they were all afraid of what they might find.

Finally, Silvermist broke the silence. "You know, I was just thinking, if Tink were here, how *not* quiet it would be right now. I really miss her."

"Yeah," Iridessa added. "Even slopping through the mud, she'd find some way to have fun."

Rosetta playfully jumped in front of the group. "Okay, okay, who am I?" She held her breath, put her hands on her hips, and strained until her face turned bright red.

"Aye," Bobble said, pointing, "that's the exact shade!"

Even Vidia laughed along with the others. It was a dead-on impression of Tinker Bell when her temper got the better of her.

Bobble shook his head, chuckling. "Quite a lot of spirit in that little tinker. Aye, a special one indeed."

Everyone laughed, but as the laughter died down and they walked on, the group grew silent and worried again.

"I'm sure she knows we're coming for her," Fawn said finally.

"I just hope we're not too late," Rosetta said, giving voice to what they all were thinking but were afraid to say.

Vidia flinched and bit her lip to keep from crying out. Silvermist noticed her distress. "Vidia?"

Vidia came to a stop. She couldn't go on any longer. The others needed to hear the truth. "Listen," she said, "there's something you all should know."

Rain kept pouring down harder than ever. Vidia's wings felt as heavy as her heart. She looked at the wet, bedraggled band of rescue fairies and felt almost too ashamed to go on. But she did. "Tinker Bell getting trapped is all my fault," she choked out.

Every fairy drew in a breath.

"I slammed the door of that little house on Tinker Bell to teach her a lesson, and . . . I tried to get her out, but the door was stuck. I tried, but I couldn't," Vidia confessed. "And now I've put us all in danger. I am so sorry."

She felt an arm softly circle her shoulder. Another hand squeezed her arm. Vidia lifted her head and saw that they had all moved closer to comfort her.

Rosetta fixed her with a sympathetic eye. "Honey, this is not your fault. We all know that Tinker Bell can get in plenty of trouble all by herself."

Iridessa nodded. "It scares me to think what would have happened if you hadn't been there, Vidia."

Vidia was speechless. Sympathy. Understanding. Forgiveness. She'd always thought those things were for the other fairies—the ones who couldn't fly fast, the ones who made mistakes. Not for her.

"I don't know what to say," she whispered.

Rosetta smiled. "How about . . ." She thrust out her hand. "Faith . . ."

Together, Iridessa and Fawn added their hands to the pile and spoke in unison. ". . . trust . . ."

Vidia thrust her hand in and they all finished the pledge together. ". . . and pixie dust!" they shouted gleefully.

Vidia's heart soared with renewed energy and enthusiasm. For the first time ever, she felt as if she had real friends. And it felt good.

Nearby, Clank was struggling to climb a wall-like pile of rocks.

"Can you reach it, Clanky?" Bobble asked.

"Almost," Clank grunted. "Just a little more . . ."

Bobble walked over to him so Clank could stand on his shoulders. Clank's head rose over the top of the rocks.

“Now can you see anything?” Bobble groaned.

“No,” Clank said. “There’s a big building in the way.”

“Building?” Bobble repeated, trying to think what Clank meant. Then he understood. “It’s a house!” he shouted happily. “That’s it, Clanky. We got it!”

“What’ve we got?” Clank asked.

“House . . . House . . . Get off,” Bobble groaned, his knees beginning to buckle under Clank’s weight.

“Oh, sorry,” Clank said.

“I can’t feel my legs,” Bobble wailed.

But Vidia’s legs wanted to dance, because she knew they had done it. Against all odds, they had found their way back to the human house—and to Tinker Bell.

Inside her room, Lizzy lay on her bed with her head buried under a pillow. Tink fluttered beside her. “I’m so sorry, Lizzy,” she jingled.

Tinker Bell couldn't tell if Lizzy understood or not, but at least she began to speak. "I'm so glad you're here. You're my best friend."

That made Tinker Bell feel worse. Lizzy's father should be her best friend, not a visiting fairy. Lizzy pulled her head out from under the pillow and opened the fairy field journal. "You want to hear a secret?"

Tinker Bell leaned closer, indicating that she did.

"It's something I've never told anyone before."

Tinker Bell flew near Lizzy's lips so she could hear her whisper.

"I wish I were a fairy," Lizzy confided. "Just like you. Then I could help the flowers bloom, and talk to the animals, and fly around with the other fairies all the time. That would be fun."

Lizzy's secret gave Tinker Bell an idea. She grabbed Lizzy's finger and led her to the middle of the room.

"Where are we going?" Lizzy asked.

Tinker Bell pantomimed for Lizzy to open her arms and close her eyes. As soon as Lizzy's lashes fluttered down, Tinker Bell flew above her head and shook a big handful of pixie dust all over her.

Tinker Bell laughed as she watched the pixie dust take effect. Lizzy's pigtails floated upward first. Then Lizzy herself. Her eyes flew open and she let out a shriek as she floated higher, grabbing wildly for the bedpost. She clutched it with both hands.

Lizzy grinned from ear to ear. *Wheeee!* She opened her arms like Tink and took an exploratory flight across the room.

Lizzy did fine—at first. But she soon lost control and flipped over several times before crashing into a bookshelf. *"Whoaaa! Ouch!"*

For the next attempt, Tinker Bell gave Lizzy a little tug. Lizzy went bouncing from one wall to the next, with a short sprint across the ceiling. "Oh, my! I'm flying." Lizzy giggled gleefully. "Look at me! I'm a fairy!"

Fifteen

The rescue party had finally arrived.

Once they had sneaked into the kitchen, Vidia filled them in on the layout of the house. "Tinker Bell is upstairs," she told them. "The little girl has her in a cage."

"In a cage!" Rosetta cried.

"There's also a large human man in the house who doesn't like creatures with wings. He pins them up in a display case."

"Great," Fawn said dryly. "Anything else?"

Vidia tried for an airy tone. "Oh, yes. The cat."

"The cat!" Iridessa yelped. "What cat?"

Before Vidia could answer, she saw Clank and Bobble pointing nervously toward the doorway and backing away.

"That cat!" the two of them wailed together.

Mr. Twitches came stalking in, huge, hairy, wet, and mad. A flash of lightning behind him made him look even more evil than usual.

"Fawn?" Bobble prompted.

"You're an animal fairy," Rosetta reminded her.

Fawn shook her head. "I can reason with bunnies and squirrels, but not Mr. Soggy-Bottom."

Mr. Twitches bared his teeth and prepared to pounce.

"Run!" Fawn yelled.

Mr. Twitches leapt, and the fairies ran toward a nearby broomstick. They raced up the broomstick and jumped from the top of the broom to the bottom of a coat hanging on a nearby peg. They quickly climbed up the coat and hopped to the safety of a high shelf full of dishes—*all except Clank!*

Heavy Clank panted and gasped as he struggled to haul his bulk up the coat.

"Clank!" Silvermist warned as Mr. Twitches circled

underneath the coat with his eyes on the vulnerable tinker.

Bobble leaned down and stuck his hand out for Clank to grab.

Too late!

Mr. Twitches sprang, flinging himself at the coat. His claws sank into the cloth. The cat's weight began to pull him downward.

Clank was launched into the air and landed inside a teacup on a shelf. His bag of pixie dust broke, and sparkling dust fell everywhere. "I'm okay," he assured them.

Vidia pointed to the stairway in the hall outside the kitchen. "We still need to get to that stairway," she said.

They would have to cross the kitchen. Mr. Twitches paced back and forth on the floor, looking up at them and plotting his next move.

"If we could just build a bridge or something," Silvermist said.

"That's it!" Bobble said. "A bridge!" Then he paused,

thinking hard. "But a bridge made out of . . . what?"

"Uh, guys!" Clank said in a worried voice.

Vidia and the others were still pondering their tactics.

"Guys," Clank repeated.

Vidia glanced up and gasped. All of the cups, plates, and silverware in the kitchen, which had been sprinkled with Clank's pixie dust, were now hovering slightly above the shelves. Vidia's eyes widened. "Clank! You're a genius!"

Clank blinked, wondering what he could possibly have done to win Vidia's approval. "Huh?" Then he saw what she had in mind. "Oh," he began. A floating plate smacked him in the head. "It was nothing," he groaned.

"All right!" Vidia said enthusiastically. "Let's do this."

The fairies made a floating bridge out of plates and saucers. They began crossing the room. But then Mr. Twitches took his own flying leap and landed on a plate in the middle of the bridge, sending cups and saucers spinning in every direction.

The fairies hung on for dear life, clinging to the cups and saucers as they spun around the kitchen like an amusement park ride.

Vidia was thrown off her plate but managed to grab on to a floating fork. The fork spun across the kitchen, carried Vidia into the hall, and came to a stop against a light fixture near the stairs.

Fawn, still hanging on to her own plate, flew past a plant on the windowsill. "Rosetta!" she called out to the garden fairy. "Is this what I think it is?"

Rosetta looked over and began to beam. "Darling, that's *exactly* what you think it is. Catnip!" She shouted to Vidia, still watching from the hallway. "You get to Tink and we'll take care of the cat."

"Got it!" Vidia shouted back. She pushed off from the wall, riding her floating fork, and surfed to the bottom of the stairs just as Dr. Griffiths came out of his office.

Vidia veered to miss him and dropped into the shadows.

Dr. Griffiths began to climb the stairs. As soon as his back was safely to her, Vidia began climbing them herself . . . one step at a time.

Sixteen

Upstairs, Tinker Bell was still giving Lizzy a flying lesson.

There was a knock on the door, and they both froze.

"Lizzy!"

Lizzy struggled to land. "Coming, Father."

"Lizzy!" he repeated.

Lizzy held on to the furniture to pull herself down and hurried to open the door. "Why, hello, Father. May I help you?" Her voice sounded too innocent, the voice of a child who was hiding something.

"What's going on in here?" Dr. Griffiths asked.

"Nothing," Lizzy answered in the same too-innocent tone.

Dr. Griffiths walked into the room. "Nothing? It sounds

like a herd of elephants have been marching up here."

Tinker Bell darted into the fairy house, where she could hide and watch.

Dr. Griffiths looked around the room, his eyes taking in the piles of fallen books, the tumbled boxes on the floor, and the crooked lampshades. "Look at this room! It looks like a cyclone hit it."

"It's not that bad," Lizzy argued.

"Not that bad? Your books are all over the floor. Your toys are everywhere. You tore your curtains." He pointed upward. "How did you get footprints on the *ceiling*?"

Lizzy looked up, and so did Tink. Sure enough, there they were. Footprints on the ceiling. Lizzy couldn't help grinning.

Big mistake.

Dr. Griffiths glowered. "This is simply too much. A temper tantrum of this magnitude is unacceptable."

"But I wasn't having a tantrum," Lizzy protested.

"Then how did this happen? The truth this time."

"Well, I . . . I . . ." Lizzy swallowed a big gulp of air. "I was flying!" she blurted out.

"You were what?"

"Flying. My fairy showed me how."

"Really? You have a real fairy living in your room?"

"Yes. And I can prove it. Just look at the research we did." Lizzy grabbed the fairy field journal and thrust it into his hands.

Dr. Griffiths flipped through it with poorly disguised contempt. "Oh, Elizabeth! This is what you've been doing? Field journals are supposed to be filled with facts. Not fairy tales."

"These *are* facts!" Lizzy argued.

Dr. Griffiths angrily shut the journal. "I don't understand this foolishness, Lizzy. You have such talent. Why would you waste it this way?"

He marched over to the wall and began tearing down

Lizzy's fairy art gallery. He crumpled one picture after the other.

"Father, wait!"

"I know this is difficult for you to understand. But this is all make-believe."

"No!" Lizzy cried. "They're real."

"Elizabeth, this discussion is over." He picked up the fairy field journal and dropped it into the trash.

Tink saw Lizzy's sad face turn to despair. "But, Father . . ." Lizzy's voice broke with a sob.

That did it. Lizzy needed to stand up to this big human bully of a father. Safe or not, it was time to help her out.

Tinker Bell zoomed out of the fairy house and hovered right in front of Dr. Griffiths's nose. She glowered and shook her fist. She didn't care that he couldn't understand what she was saying—Tinker Bell wasn't about to let anything stop her!

Dr. Griffiths froze. He stumbled backward and fell onto

Lizzy's bed. "It . . . it . . . can't be!" he whispered.

He stared, as if in shock. Tinker Bell hoped he was suitably intimidated and impressed. She did a couple of figure eights so he could really see her in action. After making a neat landing on the table, she struck a "ta-da" pose.

"It's okay, Father. She won't hurt you." Lizzy took Dr. Griffiths by the hand and led him to the table where Tinker Bell stood.

Dr. Griffiths knelt down beside the table, his expression changing from shock to wonder. "It's . . . it's . . . extraordinary."

"Aren't her wings beautiful?" Lizzy sighed.

"Yes," he agreed. "Very similar to *Apoidea*. Or, no, no, *Odonata*. Look at the limb proportionality to the cranial radius. Fascinating."

And with that, he lifted his arm. He was holding a jar. He was planning to trap Tink.

"Tink! Watch out!" cried a familiar voice.

Tinker Bell turned around, stunned. "Vidia? What are you doing here?"

"Get out of the way!" Vidia yelled.

Just as the jar was about to come down on top of Tink, Vidia slammed right into her. She knocked Tink clean off the table and sent her flying into a pile of books.

Blam!

Vidia was inside the jar. She had pushed Tinker Bell out of the way and let herself be trapped.

And it had all happened so fast, Dr. Griffiths didn't realize he had captured a completely different fairy.

Seventeen

Tinker Bell saw Dr. Griffiths cranking up his automobile. And she saw Vidia, inside the jar, fluttering helplessly.

Vidia had put herself in danger to save Tinker Bell. Saving Vidia was now up to Tinker Bell.

"Father, you can't do this!" Lizzy called out.

But her father refused to listen. "Lizzy, I don't have much time. The trustees will only wait for me until nine o'clock. Please go back in the house." The engine sprang to life with a great roar. Dr. Griffiths jumped into the driver's seat, threw the car into gear, and drove away at top speed.

Tinker Bell zoomed out of the bedroom and down the stairs and was just entering the kitchen when Lizzy came into the room. "Tinker Bell. I'm so sorry. My father's taking your friend to the city. I tried to stop him, but he just wouldn't listen."

Before Tinker Bell could say a word, there was a happy-sounding *"Meooww"* from the hallway.

Tink and Lizzy turned to see where it came from and saw Fawn, Rosetta, Iridessa, Silvermist, Clank, and Bobble come riding into the kitchen on Mr. Twitches's back.

"Tinker Bell!" they all shouted with glee.

The group hopped off the blissfully happy kitty—still full of catnip—and sent him on his way.

"Tinker Bell. You okay, Sweet Pea?" Rosetta asked.

"What happened?" asked Silvermist. "Where's Vidia?"

Tinker Bell was happy to see her friends, but she didn't have time to celebrate. "Lizzy's father trapped Vidia in a jar while she was saving me," she told them breathlessly. "We have to hurry and rescue her!"

There was a pause while this information sank in. "It's still raining," Iridessa pointed out.

Tink tapped her chin, thinking. "We can't fly, but I think I know somebody who can."

Lizzy stood in the middle of the kitchen while the fairies flew around her. They helped her into her rain slicker and hat.

Lizzy chewed nervously on her lip. "I'm scared, Tinker Bell. Floating around my room is one thing, but flying all the way to London?"

Tinker Bell lifted Lizzy's chin as if to say "No problem."

"That easy, huh?" Lizzy's tone said she wasn't really convinced. But she managed a little salute. "Okay. Okay. I'll be brave."

"All right, fairies," Tinker Bell instructed, "we need all the pixie dust we can get. This girl's got a long journey ahead of her."

Lizzy opened her arms and the fairies flew around her, each contributing his or her own precious pixie dust. They sprinkled and sprinkled until Lizzy's rain slicker twinkled and shone.

Lizzy rose into the air. Tink flew up and nestled under the collar of her coat. "All aboard!" Tink told them.

The other fairies climbed into Lizzy's pockets.

"Whoa! This better work." Lizzy picked up speed as she headed toward the kitchen door.

Bam!

Lizzy missed the door and rammed into a ceiling beam. "Oops. Sorry, fairies."

Lizzy corrected herself. On her second try, she flew cleanly through the door. Outside, she was unsteady at first, but her flying grew stronger and more confident as they flew through the storm and over the fields.

Tinker Bell was proud of her student, and her student was having a ball. "*Whoa!* I'm doing it! I'm flying!" Lizzy widened her arms and picked up speed, lowered her head, and went spiraling up into the stormy sky.

Tinker Bell looked down from her perch beneath Lizzy's collar. It had taken a while to catch up to Dr. Griffiths, but now Lizzy was doing a great job following his car. They soared across London Bridge, past Big Ben, and through the twisting city streets.

Dr. Griffiths was driving quite fast, clearly in a rush to reach the museum.

"Tinker Bell!" Lizzy cried. "I can't keep up. He's going too fast."

"Don't worry," Tink said. "I think I know how to stop him." She darted out from beneath Lizzy's collar and hurtled toward the car.

Tinker Bell took a couple of deep breaths, flew under the

car to the engine, and balanced on it. Chugging machinery pounded around her. She saw a glass oil pot. If she could knock it over, she could probably stop the car. She reached out to topple it, but it wouldn't budge.

She climbed down a copper tube through the maze of pumping machinery. When she spotted something sparkly, her tinker's intuition kicked in.

Something told her that whatever that sparkly thing was, it was probably what made this huge machine go. Because if there's one thing fairies know, it's this: *If it sparkles, it's important*.

Moving stealthily forward, she examined the wires leading to the sparkly thing. With all her might, she pulled on the lead wire. It gave, but not much.

Tinker Bell yanked harder.

Again, it gave. But it didn't break.

Tinker Bell gritted her teeth. She let go of the copper tube so she could pull with both hands. She beat her wings furiously so she could hover upside down. And on the count of three, she gave a tremendous tug.

The response was *huge*!

There was a hideous, horrible noise, and a burst of electricity arced across the engine, barely missing Tinker Bell.

The car came to a skidding stop, and Tink was flung from beneath it. She turned over and over, finally coming safely out of her spin.

She saw Dr. Griffiths beating his hands against the wheel of the stopped car. "No! No! No! No!"

He realized that the automobile was out of commission. But he wasn't finished yet. He jumped out of the car and continued down the street on foot.

Tinker Bell could see the jar in his hands.

This guy was really beginning to get on her nerves. He was as relentless as Mr. Twitches.

Tink could feel her face turning red with anger.

She followed Dr. Griffiths down the street and up the steps of the London Museum. He had his hand on the door when a voice rang out overhead.

"Father!"

Dr. Griffiths came to a surprised stop.

Eighteen

"Father! Father! Don't take her in there."

Dr. Griffiths looked up and saw Lizzy soaring overhead, trailing a sparkling cloud of pixie dust.

He reeled back, amazed. "What in the world . . . ?"

Lizzy floated down and hovered beside him.

"Lizzy!" he breathed. "You . . . you . . . you're . . . *flying*!"

"Yes, I am."

"But how? How are you doing that?"

Tinker Bell flew up near Lizzy's face as she alighted on the ground.

"My friends showed me how."

One by one, all of the fairies emerged from the pockets

and folds of Lizzy's rain slicker. After their long ride under cover, they were dry enough to fly again.

"I don't understand," Dr. Griffiths said plaintively.

"You don't have to understand," Lizzy told him kindly. "You just have to believe."

Slowly, so as not to frighten him, the fairies flew closer to Dr. Griffiths, circling him and illuminating him with the glow of pixie dust.

"I do believe," he said softly. "I do believe."

Dr. Griffiths opened his arms, inviting Lizzy to rush into them for a big hug. "Oh, Lizzy, I'm so sorry. So very sorry. I'll never doubt you again."

After a few moments, he let her go and held up the jar. He began to open it, then held it out to Lizzy. "Will you do the honors?"

Lizzy eagerly accepted the jar and opened the top. Vidia flew out at once and immediately found herself engulfed in a group fairy hug.

"Vidia!" Tinker Bell exclaimed happily.

The fairies celebrated by frolicking in a circle around Dr. Griffiths and Lizzy, turning their little orbit bright with joy.

Then the fairies began sprinkling the humans with clouds of sparkling, twinkling fairy dust.

"Whoaaaa! Whoaaa!" Dr. Griffiths cried in alarm and wonder as he and Lizzy began to rise into the air. "*Whoooaaaa!* Careful!"

"Lift your arms!" Lizzy instructed. "And kick your feet!"

Dr. Griffiths slowly raised his arms and hesitantly kicked his feet.

Lizzy shouted encouragement. "You're doing it, Father! You're doing it!"

Dr. Griffiths's face broke into a broad grin. "Why, I think I'm getting the hang of it. Yes. Why, I'm *flying*!" he shouted, his voice full of joy. This was amazing!

Soon he and Lizzy were swooping and capering through the sky over London.

Tinker Bell sat cross-legged on the edge of a red-and-white-checkered cloth. Not far away sat Dr. Griffiths and Lizzy.

"Hey, Tink." Vidia flew down and sat beside her. "So, you ever been to one of these before?"

"Yeah," Tinker Bell answered. "Once. It's pretty fun."

"What are you supposed to do?" Vidia asked.

"Oh, it's easy," Tinker Bell explained. "You just pick this up." She picked up a tiny teacup and motioned to Vidia to do the same. Vidia picked up another cup and looked again at Tinker Bell for instruction.

"You hold it out . . ."

"Got it."

"Now, just raise your pinky, like this." Tinker Bell extended her pinky finger, and Vidia did the same.

"Then you say"—Tinker Bell mimicked Lizzy's prim tea party voice—"Excuse me, Miss. May I have a spot of tea?"

Lizzy stood by, ready with the pot. When she saw Tinker Bell's raised cup, she knelt down and poured a tiny splash of tea. "Why, certainly, Miss Bell. A nice fresh cup."

Vidia held out her cup of tea and repeated the words in the same funny, prim tone. "Excuse me, Miss. May I have a spot of tea?"

"But of course you may have one, too. This is a tea party, after all."

Dr. Griffiths held out his cup. "How about a cup for me, Miss Griffiths?"

Tinker Bell was very proud of Dr. Griffiths. He'd come a long way in a short time. Not only did he believe in fairies now, he also believed in playing, spending time with Lizzy, and dressing up for tea parties. He wore a spotless white suit in honor of the occasion. And he hadn't said one word about work.

Lizzy poured tea for her father. "Why, of course, Doctor. It's my pleasure, I'm sure." Then she reached for the sugar. "Would you like one lump or two?"

"Make mine three," Dr. Griffiths said with a laugh.

Cheese the mouse came forward, pulling a cart full of sugar cubes. Blaze the firefly swooped in to do the honors. He scooped up a cube and dropped it into Dr. Griffiths's cup.

Everyone had been invited to the tea party, and Lizzy and her father had provided wonderful refreshments—bowls of strawberries, plates full of cakes, and teeny-tiny fairy-sized sandwiches.

Tinker Bell and Vidia both took a sip of their tea and watched Lizzy and her father giggle together.

"Beautiful sight, isn't it?" Vidia said.

"Nothing more beautiful in the whole wide world," Tinker Bell agreed.

She thought, but didn't say, that if anyone had told her a week ago that she and Vidia would be the best of friends, or even that Vidia would take an interest in someone else, she wouldn't have believed it. Maybe summer had a magic all its own.

Suddenly, they heard a noise. A loud whistle. Louder than any whistle Tink had ever heard.

Tinker Bell's head snapped around. She'd heard about something called a railway train, but she'd never seen one.

"Don't even think about it," Vidia said without looking up from her tea.

Tinker Bell smiled and settled back down. Vidia was right—she'd done enough exploring for one trip. Besides, she didn't want to miss the story Dr. Griffiths was reading aloud from the fairy book.

Fairies settled on his shoulder and his shoes. They

perched on the teapot and on Lizzy's head—all of them drawn to the happy scene and the power of a good fairy story.

"'There are fairies to be found all over the world,'" Dr. Griffiths read. "'Fairies who have very special talents. Fairies living in trees and in the woods. There are water fairies and garden fairies and light fairies. The animal fairies help all the woodland creatures. The river fairies teach the fish to swim. The flower fairies help the flowers to bloom, and the rainbow fairies bring color to the world.'"

Tink felt a tap on her shoulder. She turned and felt a rush of happiness. It was Terence. He quietly sat down beside her. "Well, Tink," he said. "You found something to fix after all."

Tinker Bell grinned, and so did Terence. "Yeah!" she said happily. "I guess I did."

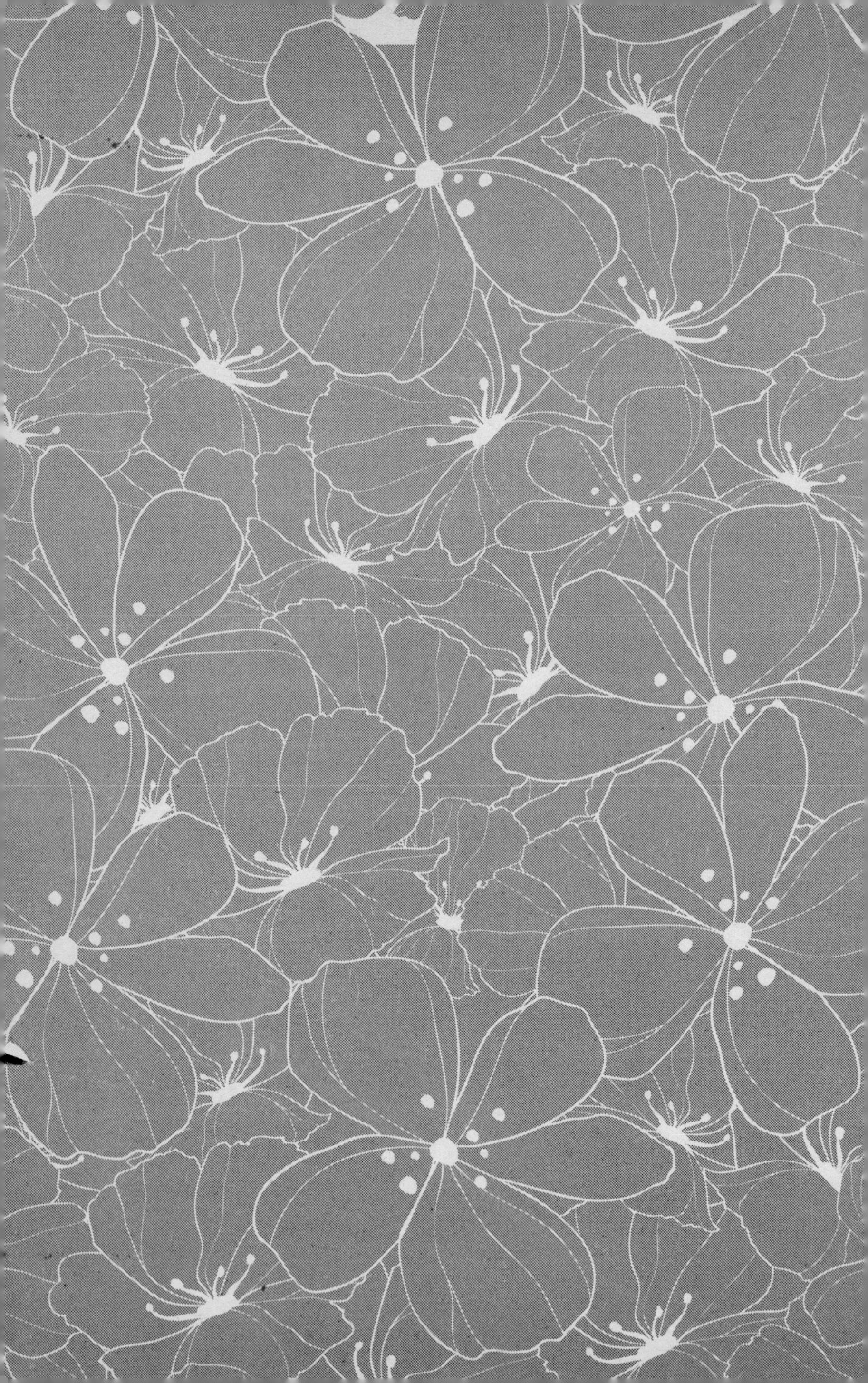